Runaway Angel

Created & Written by MISTY TAGGART
Illustrated by KAREN BELL

WORD
Kids!

WORD PUBLISHING
Dallas·London·Vancouver·Melbourne

Behind the third cloud to the right,
just around the corner from the rainbow, is the Angel Academy.
This is where young angels learn to be real guardian angels.

Text © 1995 by Susan Misty Taggart. Illustrations © 1995 by Karen Bell.
Trademark application has been filed on the following: The Angel Academy ™, StarCentral™,
Angel Heaven™, Jubilate™, Mirth™, Angelus™, Stella the Starduster™, Astrid™, Staria™, Miss Celestial™, Puffaluff™.

Managing Editor: Laura Minchew   *Project Editor:* Beverly Phillips

Library of Congress Cataloging-in-Publication Data

Taggart, Misty, 1940–
   Runaway angel/created & written by Misty Taggart;
illustrated by Karen Bell.
    p.   cm. (The angel academy; #6)
   "Word kids!"
   Summary: Tired of waiting for her wings to grow enough so that she can get an Earth Assignment, Mirth decides that
she does not want to be an angel-in-training any more—until she discovers a little girl who needs her help.
   ISBN 0-8499-5085-6 (pbk.)
   [1. Guardian angels—Fiction. 2. Angels—Fiction. 3. Self-acceptance—Fiction. 4. Patience—Fiction.] I. Bell, Karen, 1949– ill.
II. Title III. Series: Taggart, Misty, 1940– Angel academy; #6.
PZ7.T1284Ru 1995
[E]—dc20
       94-45098
       CIP
       AC

Printed in the United States of America   95 96 97 98 99 00 LBM 9 8 7 6 5 4 3 2 1

STARIA
She thinks she's very grown-up, but don't you believe it.

ASTRID
Her laugh is as big as her sweet tooth.

ANGELUS
If you have a question about anything, he has the answer—he thinks.

JUBILATE
He's ready to right every wrong—and has a lot of fun doing it.

MIRTH
She may be small, but she can be big trouble.

BEEP! BEEP!

"Look, it's Angel Abigail in her Cloudmobile," called Astrid. She and Jubilate were hurrying to The Angel Academy.

"And Mirth's with her!" added Jubilate.

Mirth made Angel Abigail feel young. And Abigail made Mirth feel special.

"I wish I didn't have to go to school." (Mirth would much rather spend the day with her friend Angel Abigail.) "I never get to go on Earth Assignments," the little angel sighed.

Mirth's teacher, Miss Celestial, had told Mirth her wings were still far too small to fly her from Earth back to Angel Heaven.

"Why don't my wings grow faster?"

"Don't be in such a hurry to grow up," Angel Abigail remarked.

"It's no fun being the littlest," Mirth pouted.

This week had been especially hard for Mirth.

On Monday, Jubilate and Astrid had gone to Earth.

And on Tuesday, Staria went down the Big Cloud Slide to Earth.

Then, on Wednesday, Angelus flew to Earth.

And each time Mirth was left behind.

"Miss Celestial probably won't let me go to Earth today, either," Mirth complained.

Later, in class, Mirth just couldn't keep her mind on her studies. And Puffaluff, her pet cloud, wasn't helping one bit. He kept making funny faces through the classroom window.

"Shoo! Get out of here, Puff!" said Miss Celestial. Their teacher was about to close the window when Jedediah the Operator of StarCentral rode up on his bike. He gave her another Earth Assignment.

"Oh, please let me go!" Mirth called hopefully. Maybe this assignment would be hers.

"Your wings still aren't quite big enough," said Miss Celestial. "Be patient. They'll grow."

Mirth fluttered her little wings. "It's taking *too* long!" Then she announced, "I don't want to be a guardian angel!"

Well, *that* surprised everyone. . . . Angelus dropped his calculator! Astrid's glasses slid off her nose! Jubilate's halo popped right off his head! And Staria's hat slipped down over her eyes!

Before Miss Celestial could say a word, Mirth ran out of the room.

Puffaluff flew Mirth to see her good friend Angel Abigail. The older angel told her, "I'm sorry, Mirth, but no one can make your wings grow any faster."

"Then I don't want to be a guardian angel!" Mirth stomped her foot on the clouds. "I'm going to run away!" And off she went before Angel Abigail could stop her.

Mirth was halfway down the Cloud Slide to Earth when she heard the familiar, *BEEP! BEEP!* It was Angel Abigail in her Cloudmobile.

"Let's run away together. Hop in!" said Mirth's friend. And in the twinkle of a star, the two were heading down through the clouds to Earth.

As the Cloudmobile landed in the middle of Plumrose Lane and Buttercup Road, the most amazing thing happened. The car's wings disappeared—and so did Mirth's and Angel Abigail's! And with a *POOF!* even their halos vanished! (This always happened when grown-up angels came to Earth. But it never happened to guardian angels-in-training.)

Mirth was startled. "My wings are gone!" Abigail laughed "Well, two angels riding down the street in a Cloudmobile most certainly would cause a traffic jam. Besides, I thought you didn't want to be an angel."

"I don't! I'm glad my wings are gone," Mirth said.

As they drove by a park, Mirth heard some children laughing. "Oh, let's stop," she said. After thinking a moment, she asked Angel Abigail, "Will they all be able to see me?"

"Why, of course. Remember, you wished not to be an angel anymore."

Mirth happily ran off to play with the Earth children.

Mirth was having fun playing games and making friends.

"Let's play hide-and-seek," suggested one of the little girls. Mirth and the others found hiding places. Mirth hid behind a large, old tree.

As she waited, Mirth saw a little girl crying. She looked very frightened. "What's wrong?" Mirth asked.

"I'm lost," the little girl cried. "I got mad at my mother, and I ran away. Now I don't know how to get back home."

The little girl's name was Lucinda. She was five years old.

"I'll help you. You see, I'm really an—" Mirth suddenly stopped as she remembered she wasn't an angel any longer. "Don't cry. We'll find your house, together," she promised Lucinda.

If Mirth had been sent to Earth as Lucinda's guardian angel-in-training, she would have known just how to help the little girl. But Mirth wasn't an angel any longer.

Well, with or without her wings, Mirth was determined to help Lucinda get back home.

With Angel Abigail following in her Cloudmobile, Mirth and Lucinda searched the neighborhood. They hoped Lucinda would see something familiar. After a while, the two new friends stopped to share Mirth's rainbow jam sandwich on star-crust bread.

"When you're with me, I'm not so scared," said Lucinda. Mirth liked that.

Meanwhile, back in Angel Heaven everyone was concerned about Mirth. "Where could she have gone?" asked Miss Celestial.

Then George the Heavenly Handyman looked over the edge of a cloud. He smiled and said, "We can stop looking."

On Earth, it was getting dark and Lucinda wished she were at home in her own room.

"Oh, Mirth, you promised you'd help me get back home," said Lucinda.

"I'm trying," Mirth sighed. Oh, how she wanted to have her wings back!

Nearby, Angel Abigail was surprised when a cheerful policeman walked up to her car. "Evening, Abigail," he said, with a twinkle in his eye. Abigail smiled as she recognized the familiar face as Geroge from Angel Heaven.

"Would you keep an eye on those two little ones?" she asked. "I'll be right back."

Mirth and Lucinda were relieved to see the friendly policeman. "My friend is lost, and I'm trying to help her get home," Mirth told him.

"Well, aren't you a sweet little angel," he said. Mirth blinked. He had called her an angel. How could he know? . . . Just then, Mirth heard the familiar *BEEP! BEEP!*

Up drove Angel Abigail. And sitting in the seat next to her was Lucinda's mother.

"How did you find her?" Mirth asked Angel Abigail.

"Angels know just where to look," Abigail smiled.

Mirth was so happy for Lucinda.

"If I still had my wings, I could have helped Lucinda," Mirth said. She turned to thank the friendly policeman, but he was gone.

"I do miss Angel Heaven," sighed Mirth. "I'm sorry I ran away." Looking toward heaven, Mirth whispered, "Please, could I have my wings back?" And with a *TWINKLE* Mirth's tiny wings reappeared.

"Oh, look, my wings are back!"

Wings also returned to Angel Abigail and her Cloudmobile. Then the shiny car lifted up, up through the clouds toward Angel Heaven.

Mirth was so glad to be home and to have her wings back. "But it's still no fun being the littlest," she said.

"Come with me," smiled Angel Abigail. And she took Mirth to The Angel Academy Pre-School. It was filled with happy, giggling angel babies.

"I'm not the littlest angel-in-training, after all!" Mirth gave Angel Abigail a big hug. "I won't ever run away again," the little angel promised. "I want Miss Celestial to teach me to be the very best guardian angel ever."

Look for these and other ANGEL ACADEMY™ books and products

at your favorite bookstore, gift shop, and retailer:

The Staria Dress-Up Set With Book
by Daval International, LTD.

Angel Parade Pileup

Sister, Stay Out!

The Razzleberry Rescue

The Angel Academy: A Collection of Modern Angel Tales

Don't miss the fun! Join THE ANGEL ACADEMY™ KIDS CLUB.

A one-year membership includes a Welcome Packet of fun sent directly from Angel Heaven. You'll get a Club Membership I.D. Card, Angel Academy Surprises and Special Offers throughout the year, and a special Birthday Surprise!

For a one-year membership, send the completed registration form along with a check or money order for $10.00, per child, ($13.00 in Canada) to:

THE ANGEL ACADEMY™ KIDS CLUB
P.O. Box 39480
Membership Dept.
Phoenix, AZ 85069–9480

Please allow 6–8 weeks for delivery. Subject to change without notice. AZ residents add sales tax.

The Angel Academy Kids Club is a division of Estee Productions, Inc.

Do not tear out this page from your book. Photocopy the form below or use a clean sheet of paper and PRINT the following information:

Child's Name: _____ Girl ❏   Boy ❏

Address: _____

City: _____ State: _____ ZIP: _____

Phone: (_____) _____ Age: _____ Birthdate: _____